For the writers:
Sally, Valerie, Vera and, always, Henrietta,
with love and chocolate biscuits
S.H.

To William, Henry and Elinor
K.P.

British Library Cataloguing Publication Data
A catalogue record of this book is available from the British Library.

HB ISBN 0 340 77412 6
PB ISBN 0 340 77413 4

Text copyright © Sandra Ann Horn 2000
Illustrations copyright © Karen Popham 2000

The right of Sandra Ann Horn to be identified as the author and Karen Popham
to be identified as the illustrator of this Work has been asserted by them in
accordance with the Copyright, Designs and Patents Act 1988.

First hb edition published 2000
First pb edition published 2000

1 3 5 7 9 10 8 6 4 2

Published by Hodder Children's Books
a division of Hodder Headline Limited
338 Euston Road London NW1 3BH

Designed by Dawn Apperley

Printed in Hong Kong

THE
TATTYBOGLE
TREE

Sandra Ann Horn and Karen Popham

Hodder
Children's
Books

A division of Hodder Headline Limited

Essie Clucket had a big red jumble-sale hat
and an old flowery frock.
She wore a sheep bell round her neck.
Her hair was a tangle of yellow wool.

Essie was supposed to frighten the birds away, but she forgot.

The birds liked to sit along her hat and listen to the sheep bell. It made music when the wind blew.

'A bird or three on a big red hat is very smart,' said Essie.

In the evening, when the birds went to roost, Essie Clucket was all by herself and she didn't like it.

'There's no one here to see my fine clothes and have a bit of a chat with,' she sighed.

'I'm here,' whispered a voice from the corner of the field.
It came from a beautiful tree with a crown of catkin buds.
　'Who might you be?' asked Essie.
　'I'm Tattybogle,' said the tree. 'I was a scarecrow once
until the wild wind blew me all to pieces and there was
nothing left but my stick. Then I grew into a tree.'

'What's it like then being a tree?' said Essie.

'Magic!' said Tattybogle. 'There's music when it rains and dancing when it's windy, but I don't get blown away. There's sun on my leaves, and nights full of stars, and a handsome lady scarecrow to pass the time of day with . . .'

Essie Clucket tossed her curls and made a little curtsy.

The days grew long and warm. The catkins on the
Tattybogle tree opened into golden tassels. Essie's hat
glowed like a poppy in the summer sun. In the evenings,
Tattybogle told Essie all about being a tree. He liked it.

'There's nothing better,' he said, 'than having your
roots deep in the earth and your head high in the sky.'

When the breeze blew, Essie rang her sheep bell and
the birds came to listen.

'They make the place so cheery,' said Tattybogle.

'And smart too,' said Essie Clucket.

It was a very hot summer.
One night, three green-white moths flew over the hedge.
They had blown in from far away, on the warm wind.
They rested a moment on Essie's hat . . .

. . . then flew to the Tattybogle tree.
They sipped the nectar from the catkins
with long curly tongues.

'Come back here!' said Essie Clucket.
'And prettify my hat!'

The moths stayed where they were.
More and more moths flew to Tattybogle.

'There's room for all,' said Tattybogle.

'There's a tidy lot of them,' said Essie. 'Couldn't you spare a few for a friend's hat?'

'They seem to like it here best,' said Tattybogle.

Essie Clucket turned her face away.

When the moths had finished drinking, they flew
under Tattybogle's leaves and laid little clumps of eggs.
There were hundreds of them. Then the moths flew away.
    'Excuse me, you've left something behind,' called
Tattybogle, but the moths were not listening.
    'There's eggs all under my leaves,' said Tattybogle.
    'Serves you right,' sulked Essie.

Tattybogle soon forgot about the eggs until, one sunny day, the eggs split open and tiny caterpillars wriggled out.

'Well I never!' said Tattybogle. 'I've never seen so many little wrigglers.'

Essie Clucket pretended not to notice. The caterpillars began to munch Tattybogle's leaves.

'I don't suppose they'll do much harm,' he said.
'They're only little.'
    The more the caterpillars ate, the more they grew.
The more they grew, the more they ate.

Tattybogle was worried.
Some parts of him
were quite bare.
His branches
drooped.

Essie Clucket stopped being cross and started to be worried too.

'You don't look too good,' she said.

Still the caterpillars munched. Tattybogle felt ill and weak and frightened. 'They are eating me to pieces!' he said.

Essie Clucket wanted to cry.

A breeze blew across the field and ruffled Essie's hair. She had an idea. She waved her arms in the breeze. The sheep bell began to chime. Birds flew in from all directions and sat along her hat.

'Are you hungry, my dears?' asked Essie.
They were always hungry.
'There are caterpillars over yonder,'
she said.
'Where, where, where?' sang the birds.
Essie swung round and pointed to the
Tattybogle tree.

The birds flew over and began to hunt.
There were caterpillars everywhere. The birds sang,
'The Tattybogle tree is the place to be! Tattypillar,
Caterbogle!'

Caterpillars were disappearing fast from Tattybogle.
He felt better.

'Thank you, Essie!' he called.

'You're welcome,' she said. 'I want the birds back when you've finished with them, mind.'

Soon the Tattybogle tree grew new leaves, and he
stretched up tall in the sun. Essie wore a mouse nest in
her hat.

The birds had not found all the caterpillars. Some had
hidden. They had tied themselves to the branches with
silken threads. They grew hard grey-brown shells. They
looked just like bumps on the bark.

When the first frosts brushed Tattybogle's leaves with
scarlet, and Essie's hat with silver, the bumps were still
there. They stayed through the winter. They were still
there in the spring.

'I wonder what they're up to?' said Tattybogle.
'I don't know, but I'm keeping my eye on them,'
said Essie Clucket.
'So are we, so are weeeee!' sang the birds along her hat.